The ABCs of Cookies

By P.J. Shaw
Illustrated by Tom Leigh

Dalmatian Press, LLC, 2007. All rights reserved.
Published by Dalmatian Press, LLC, 2008. The DALMATIAN PRESS name and logo are trademarks of Dalmatian Press, LLC, Franklin, Tennessee 37067. No part of this book may be reproduced or copied in any form without written permission from the copyright owner.

Printed in the U.S.A.
08 09 10 NGS 10 9 8 7 6 5 4 3
17302 Sesame Street 8x8 Storybook:The ABCs of Cookies

A is for **apron**, which matches this hat.

B is for **butter**, and...

You made
a tower!

D is for **dishes**.

E is for **eggs**, and...

F is for flour.

K is for **krispies** you put on the top.

L is for **lemon** juice.

O is for **oven**.

P is for **pan**. (But first put your glove on!)

R is for raisins, golden and sweet.

S is for **sprinkles**.
And now...

Time to eat!

U-m-m-m is the way
a warm cookie tastes.

V is vanilla.

Or Valentine shapes!

Z is for zero—they're all in your tummy!